JUSTINIAN APPROACH

(SHORT DRAMA)

YOUR LOVE FOR ME MUST
BE TESTED...THE
JUSTINIAN'S DECREE!

LAWSON MOTUNRAYO AUGUSTER

Justinian Approach

FOR MORE INFORMATION:

Motunrayo Lawson
Email: motunrayolawson5@gmail.com
Phone Number: +2348058092789

CONTENT

STORY CAST

The Justinian: *(Princess of the Legal kingdom)*

King Law: *(King of the Legal kingdom &father of Justinian)*

The Outlaws: *(A well-known family of the legal kingdom)*

The Prisoners of Love: *(A nick name given to Justinian's lovers)*

The People of the Legal kingdom

True love: *(Justinian's choice)*

Summary

This is the story of a Legal kingdom where there is zero tolerance for injustice and false-hood. If anyone is found wanting by Justinian; the princess of the legal kingdom, he or she will have her head chopped off by the Justinian's sword. She already has her face covered, so, she has no compassion for anyone, she only pays attention to the sensitivity of her weighing balance.

Your love for me will be tested!

CHAPTER 1

THE LEGAL KINGDOM

King law was gracefully sitting on his magnificent throne in his palace when the princess of the kingdom, Justinian, whom he adored so much seeing as she was his only child and had lost her mother, Queen grace while trying to give birth to her , due to this, the king made sure she lacked nothing . She was seen entering into the regal palace graceful and beautiful as always but looking very sad.

King Law was shocked to see his daughter in this condition, so he asked her why her countenance downcast..

King Law: my darling princess why are you looking sad?

Justinian: …..silence…..

King Law: what happened? Tell me anything you want and it is yours, even to the whole of my kingdom!!. You are my only child and I cannot permit anything to bother you so much that it will take away your joy.

Justinian: oh dad, royal majesty, king Law of the legal Kingdom. I have been accused of being too cruel to my subjects. I disguised myself and toured the whole kingdom searching for a good partner, one that would love me for who I am but…..silence… …

King Law: continue my princess what happened?

Justinian: … … … …silence… … … …

King Law: tell me now daughter. You are the royal princess and you are not supposed to beg anyone to be your partner, just point out to anyone among the nobles of this kingdom or any of the princes of the world and he is yours!

Justinian: Father I will not like to settle with the man that would like to marry me just for the sake of the legal throne. I want to marry a man the will complement me; accept me for who I am, be my true love and a lover of righteousness and justice. But father, hear what the men of your kingdom think about your Justinian.

CHAPTER 2
JUSTINIAN IN DISGUISE

Men of the Legal kingdom at the town square were seen talking about the princess of the legal kingdom and as they converse … … …

1ˢᵗ *man:* have you heard?

2ⁿᵈ *man:* heard what?

3ʳᵈ *man:* what?

4ᵗʰ *man:* what? …….What? (Response: from a crowd of about 200 men)

1ˢᵗ *man:* that our royal princess is looking for a suitor. A friend of mine that serves the royal princess had disclosed this to me.

One of the men in the crowd: who will want to marry her?

Another man in the crowd: that good for nothing girl, full of herself, shows no mercy on the convicted, just because her father had given her the authority to give judgment, she … she … she. A girl that lords herself over everyone in this kingdom. For this reason, nobody will like to be her husband.

3rd man: hmm, brave men of legal kingdom, don't you know that this is the time for us all to take over the kingdom from king law, and the time to take revenge on that good for nothing Justinian for all her cruelty? Has she not killed some of our brethren in the name of justice and righteousness?

2nd man: I understand your point my brother, for anyone who marries Justinian takes over the legal kingdom! And I wish to marry her for the sake of the throne.

3rd man: I wish I marry her so that I can destroy both king law and his useless daughter Justinian, then the whole kingdom would be ruled in my own terms and everyone will be happy.

1st man: (makes a plan): this is what would happen, we will all try to persuade the king to give us, Justinian's hand in marriage. We would ask for a wrestling contest to be done and the winner will win the princess's hand in marriage.

All the men of the kingdom at that scene seems to be so excited about this plan not knowing that Justinian had disguised herself to walk through the kingdom without being noticed and had overheard their discussion.

The princess cried bitterly while telling her father the whole plan cooked up by men of the kingdom. Her father was shocked and sad on hearing about this mischief planned by the men of the kingdom.

He used to think the people of the legal kingdom adored him and that they are happy with Justinian's wisdom and righteousness but now he knows clearly what they think of him and his beloved daughter.

CHAPTER 3
THE IMPORTANT ANNOUNCEMENT

The king pants in anger about the palace garden; thinking about the matter. A new idea dropped into his heart and he decided to use this idea to end the problem.

The king went back to his daughter's chamber to console her, light up her mood by assuring her he was going to bring an end to the problem.

Justinian told her father how worried she was about these evil men creating riots everywhere in the kingdom and poisoning the hearts of the people with toxic rumors, and eventually forcing her dad to abdicate the throne.

The king managed to calm down his worried daughter assuring her his decision to make an important announcement that will put an end to the problem and also change her life.

The following day, the king summoned everyone in his kingdom.

He wanted to make an important announcement.

Everyone got to the palace square anxious, not knowing what king law was about announce to them. The crowd murmured among themselves asking one another what the important message would be ....

Finally, when the people were calmed, the king called out the royal princess and told the people he would like to give Justinian hand in marriage to Prince Daniel of the neighboring kingdom.

The youths of the kingdom on hearing this, started murmuring. It became a terrible protest which was championed by those conspirators that led into a riot where 30 innocent people lost their lives.

At this Justinian was very angry and knew it was those selfish criminals that were already planning a big coup against her and her father that had instigated the riot so, she decided to go about the matter in her own way and asked her father for the permission to give justice to those innocent souls that where killed since no one could be arrested for murder.

… … … … … … … … … … … … … … … … … …

Justinian: Attention!! Why are you fighting and killing yourselves?

The crowd: we would not agree to this suggestion of king Law! Your husband would have to come from this kingdom!

Justinian: ok then, here is what I have decided;

"If any one of you, men of this kingdom can pass my love test he will be my husband but if any of you come for this love test and is found wanting by my weighing balance, then his head is removed by my sword. You already know me, I have zero tolerance for lies !!.

YOUR LOVE FOR ME WILL BE TESTED... THE JUSTINIAN'S WISH

Justinian had said this knowing well that only the greedy ones that were opposing her dad's decision would stand up to this challenge. And when she saw most of them coming forward, to take part in the contest, she was very pleased that she would have the opportunity to deal with those rebels once and for all.

People: murmuring among one another.

Justinian: if you agree then I will marry the winner who will be a citizen of this legal kingdom who would also become the prince of the legal throne but if not, then I will have to go for my father's choice for me.

Suddenly, a young handsome and courageous man among the crowed summoned courage and volunteered to prove to Justinian that he loves her. She was a bit confused because he looked strange and she had not seen him before, but then she concluded he was also among the greedy ones and should be punished.

CHAPTER 4

DUKE JUSTICE, THE OUTLAWS & KING LAW

The outlaws, as their nick name implies are known for their unruly behavior. They have been called outlaws after the demise of the family's patriarch known as Duke Justice and the missing of his first son known as love.

Years ago, before king Law became king and before the birth of Justinian the princess, Justice was a very respected and wealthy merchant of whose trade brought about the wealth and popularity of the legal kingdom.

Justice was a prince born to the royal family of the legal kingdom and used to be a cousin to prince Law of the royal family of the legal kingdom. They both had the same grandparents.

Their grandfather was the king of the legal kingdom, and the two cousins were raised as brothers after they both lost both their parents in a ship wreck and this made them very close and they both lived as brothers instead of cousins.

Justice had to step down for his little cousin, then prince Law, who had always wanted to be king and had followed his dream of becoming a wealthy merchant.

His trade had made the legal kingdom great and at the request of his grandfather he had been made duke of the kingdom.

Justice had two sons, his first son was known as Love which he named after his late wife, Lovett who passed away after childbirth. And the second son was borne to him by his second wife, Anna whom he named J-law.

Anna was Lovett's elder sister, and she had always wanted to be like her two sisters' Lovett and Faith, who was the eldest.

Lovett had married Justice, a very wealthy man and the duke of the legal kingdom while Faith had married king Law the 2nd of the legal kingdom. She was filled with so much envy for both of her sisters especially Faith who married king law whom she had loved so much.

Lovett always supported Faith preventing Her from falling into Anna's traps. Anna got tired of her and killed her sister after childbirth while pretending to assist her. She would have killed the new born had the elderly royal nanny, Ashy, not walked in.

Ashy, had loved Lovett like her own daughter so much that she took the responsibility of taking care of love that she had left behind.

Justice after two years was forced to marry Anna for the sake of his son Love since she pretended to love the boy so much that she could not do without him. Anna decided to do this because her other sister faith was now pregnant with king Law's first child which made king Law to love her more.

Anna got pregnant too, few months after and decided she wanted to go and take good care of her sister but before she left, she gave her husband, Justice slow poison that would kill him months after.

Meanwhile, Faith was so happy to see her sister that she threw a party to celebrate her welcome. Faith was seen all over the kingdom with her beloved no-good sister who actually came to destroy her.

Time passed and the time came for Faith to give birth, she gave birth to a bouncing baby girl whom she named Justinian and she died immediately after the birth of her baby.

It was revealed that Faith had died as a result of a particular poisonous herb that Anna used to give her whenever they took a stroll round the kingdom. She would also pretend to take the herb but would normally use the antidote later.

Anna, after her sister's death begged king Law to make her his wife so that she could take care of the little princess, but King Law refused, saying; he would never forget the love he had for Faith, therefore he would like to live by all those memories and never remarry. At this, King Law sent Anna back to her husband and got four nurses to take good care of little princess Justinian.

Meanwhile, back in Duke Justice's mansion, heartbroken Anna came back home wondering why her husband had not died yet. Not knowing that her husband had travelled outside the kingdom for treatment and had been given the antidote to clear off the poison.

At this, Justice had suspected all the servants to have poisoned him so he laid them off. When Anna got back and realized this change, she became hysteric venting her anger everywhere and on everyone.

Few months later, Ashy, the royal nanny died and Anna gave birth the following day to a son whom Justice named, J-law, blending his initial with his beloved cousin's name.

****J** – for justice then **law** after king law****

Anna ignored Love, her sister's son that she pretended to have loved so much and concentrated on her own son, J-law. Justice noticed this and employed new sets of maids to take care of the house and nurses to take care of love.

Few months later, Justice was found dead on his couch.

It was revealed that Anna his wife had secretly given him a sleeping potion and suffocated him to death. Zina, little Love's nurse had seen her doing this and had run away with the little boy before Anna could lay her hand on him.

On hearing these news, King Law was very devastated. After giving his brother a burial fit for the king, he mourned him for several months and his pains gave so much joy to Anna who felts she hadn't been able to give him a fitting reply for rejecting her.

King Law had made a thorough search for Love to no avail and after a while he believed he was probably dead. King Law had believed that his brother was killed because of his wealth by his servants and business partners and so he asked for the execution of the duke's servants 7 days after his brother's funeral.

CHAPTER 5

LOVE & ZINA

Years had gone by and Love grew up in another kingdom to be a responsible wealthy man like his father. He had been trained by his nurse, Zina whom he knew as his mother. On a cool noon, while chatting with his mom.

Love: mom; I'm thinking of building my business empires in the neighboring kingdoms, so, I have selected ten kingdoms around us.

Zina: ok son, bless you, I'm so proud of you.

Love, mentioned nine neighboring kingdoms he had already visited and how he greatly thinks that his business will thrive in those places.

He even told his mom that he had started putting some structures in place in 3 of those kingdoms. Zina was very thrilled at her son's success until Love told her that he would be traveling to a kingdom called legal to establish his business empire.

Zina, for the first time became hysteric and Love watched her in amazement. After sometime, she sat him down and told him the story of his life and why he should never go to the legal kingdom.

CHAPTER 6
"THE OUTLAWS"

J-law on the other hand, was so much pampered by his mother that he became so irresponsible. He refused to get educated and went about vandalizing people and their properties. This got to the notice of king law and he asked his mother to caution him but she only formed a fence around her son. King Law was very concerned about J-law's behavior because he had secretly planned to marry his daughter off to him and hand over the throne to him in honor of his father Justice.

Anna and his son were nicked named outlaws as King Law had a soft spot for them and always overlooked his mistakes. So, most people of the legal kingdom were very careful with them.

Anna had always stood by her son and had always tried to manipulate the king to her advantage. Her next target was fixing her son with Justinian so that she could finally lay her hands on the legal throne.

When King Law had announced that Justinian would marry anybody that passes the princesses' love test and that anyone found wanting would be killed, she became devastated.

J-law, was confident that he would win the love test and promised his mother that he would win and get the throne.

CHAPTER 7
THE PRISONERS OF LOVE

On Justinian's big day, all the love test contestants who were known as the prisoners of love (opposing the king's decision is equal to treason in the legal kingdom and the punishment was death).

Anyone who had opted to go through Justinian's love test was known as a rebel who was going against the king's decision. Most of the rebels stepped down on hearing the fate of what will happen to those who fail to pass the Justinian's test, and the fact that only one person will win was very scary to majority of them.

These prisoners were all taken to a large hall known as the secrete room were different kinds of treasures of the world can be found. Treasures such as gold, diamond, silver, rupees, and all other kinds of rear gem (little did they know that most of these treasures were fake. They were just painted stones.)

Also in this hall, different beautiful women were arrayed with a price tag on them and 3 oppressed people were seen sitting at a corner (2 sick boys with a big tight knotted dirty bag placed on their backs, their bodies covered with sores and wounds and they were dressed in rags. Also in that hall was an aged old woman who was already bending with a large mile stone placed on her back).

The prisoners of love were asked to practice how to live like a king and to look for the one thing they can find in the large room which they would use to prove their love to Justinian.

This is because this one thing which symbolizes **"LOVE"** would be weighed on the Justinian's weighing balance and if anyone is found wanting, his head would be chopped off by Justinian's sword, but if he passes the test, the treasures of the legal kingdom, Justinian and even the legal throne would belong to the winner while the rest of the rebels would either die or be sent on exile.

"YOUR LOVE FOR ME WILL BE TESTED ... ... THE JUSTINIAN'S DECREE!"

Immediately the prisoners of love entered the secret room, most of them forgot they were on mission. They were busy having fun with the beauties in the room, eating the nice food served on the large table, and also gathering as much treasure as they can find with the help of their lover girls.

Only one of them was very serious with his mission, he was actually truly in love with Justinian whose beauty had captured his heart from the moment he set his eyes on her.

He was so determined but on entering the room, he was very confused as to which treasure Justinian would like the most. He was still walking around, when he noticed the three oppressed people and went to help them.

Unknown to the prisoners of love, a secret camera had been placed in the large secret room which was meant to show the people of the kingdom who were waiting for the outcome at the palace court. Everyone including King Law saw clearly the activities that were going on at the secret room except Justinian who had her face covered holding sternly to her weighing balance and her sword of justice.

This secret lover of Justinian, who was known by the name Juslov noticed that he had not gathered any treasure to win Justinian's love he became worried and wanted to abandon these oppressed to fulfill his mission but these people cried out in pain and his compassion for them was more than his mission.

There was a lot of murmuring at the palace court as the whole kingdom were wandering what would become of those prisoners of love that were acting foolishly.

Most of these prisoners of love decided to run off with their new found lovers not knowing that those beautiful women were palace soldiers who led them to the palace dungeon instead of escaping with them like they thought. Immediately they got to the dungeon, they realized that they had been trapped but there was no way out for them as seventeen of the twenty contestants were guilty of this and were locked up in prison.

The remaining three contestants in the secret room included; a guy named Juslov, the good looking guy Justinian was surprise to see among the defaulters, Jlaw, Justinian's cousin whom she detested so much for his unruly behaviors and a guy named Gog, who was the first man that championed the conspiracy against Justinian and her father.

At this point, the lights of the secret room suddenly went off and all the supposed treasures, beautiful women and all the nice foods were taken away leaving the secret room empty with only the three remaining contestants and the three sickly people which includes; a sickly and dirty pregnant woman, a dirty boy with down syndrome who had a dirty piggy bag hanged around his neck and a dirty old woman with a mile stone placed on her back. All these three oppressed were sitting in a corner while Juslov was attending to them.

When the power was restored, the three contestants were shocked to see the whole room empty; Juslov was very disappointed that he couldn't get any precious stone for Justinian.

Gog and Jlaw were very proud of their achievements reminding Juslov of how he had lost the battle at the first level and would be headed by Justinian because he had nothing to show for his love for Justinian.

Suddenly there was a trumpet sound and the three prisoners adjusted themselves and were ordered by the palace guards to take whatever they had gathered and follow them to the court room to be presented in front of Justinian who was already waiting for them with her waiting balance and her sword of justice.

It would take an hour and a half to reach the palace court room, Juslov was very sad and walked down the hall way like a goat destined to be slaughtered all the way thinking about his mother Zina. The three oppressed people had opted to follow him to ask the princess for mercy on his behalf.

As they were moving the oppressed boy was coming behind and all of a sudden, he fell of his balance.

None of the men turned around to help the boy, Juslov was engrossed in his thinking, Jlaw was busy planning his next move as he had promised his mom the throne.

The four soldiers were in front and were not even aware of what was happening, but Gog who was at the very rear and busy with arranging his treasures saw the boy fall off and a diamond fall off the bag hung around the boy's neck.

This diamond rolled off and stopped at Juslov's feet. The boy managed to get himself up and smiled. Juslov turned around and didn't know where the diamond came from but was very happy, he had at least found something he could present to Justinian.

They all continued with their journey but the thought that there was a lot of diamonds in the boy's bag was all that Gog could think of, so he slowed down his pace, grabbed the boy to a corner and started dragging the bag with him.

He was very shocked to see that the boy was stronger than him and was wearing a mask, he wasn't sick at all. The boy pressed a button on the bag and gave it to Gog after which he ran away from him as fast as he could.

Gog was still happy that he finally got the bag and was also shocked to see the boy running. He realized those other oppressed people could be carrying some treasures in pretense so, as he eagerly opened the piggy bag to see what was in the bag, it exploded to his face as his whole body caught fire, he died before he was rescued and the whole scene was seen by the people at the palace court room.

The terrible thing that happened to Gog shocked both Juslov and Jlaw.

The two men were finally ushered into the palace court room before the princess Justinian who would decide their fate.

Jlaw was brought forward to prove himself to Justinian who was stretching forward her weighing balance so that the contestants might have whatever they have gotten to prove their love to her weighed.

He dropped on one side of the weighing balance all the treasures he had acquired one after the other because on the other side was a diamond which Justinian had placed there to detect the value of what they have brought.

(This is because only those three oppressed people had the real treasure with them which can match up to Justinian standard treasure. These people were actually noble people in the palace who were disguised as oppressed people. Justinian had appointed them to help her screen the greedy men from the righteous ones and to know who will show them compassion and they will reward that person with the real treasure that will match up to Justinian's standard and by this Justinian will know the one who can show true kindness and be fit for the legal throne in future. She had come up with this because she had perceived all the contestants to be greedy and ruthless.)

All of Jlaw's treasures didn't affect the weighing balance since all were fake treasures and as he did that, Justinian was smiling waving her sword with the other hand. Anna (Jlaw's mother) who was sitting at the court's corner for the kingdom nobles with her jaws widely apart and her mouth in her heart watching how her son was about to be killed. All of a sudden, Jlaw brought out another treasure a diamond and immediately, the balance went down but didn't get to the gauge point. Justinian was confused and wondered who this man was, as she told him to step aside. Anna was very excited that her son was winning , King Law, most of the people of the legal kingdom and the invited nobles were shocked to see this then Justinian asked about the remaining people and the solders explained in court that they had been imprisoned for their crime leaving only one more prisoner of love to go through his test.

Justinian declared once again: ***Your love for me must be tested ----------- the Justinian's decree!***

Prisoners of love: ... ... silence ... .

Juslov stepped up for his love test challenge when he realized that his diamond had been stolen from him. He looked towards Jlaw who wickedly grin at him. (It was then he realized Jlaw had stolen the diamond from him when he was trying to rescue Gog).

Juslov went on his knees to pray Justinian for mercy when the remaining two oppressed people came to pull him up. The pregnant woman revealed she wasn't pregnant and as a matter of fact, she had placed large series of treasure which include real precious stones; diamonds, ruby, gold etc in a round bag on her belly making it look like she was pregnant. She gave this rare gem to Juslov who placed it on the weighing balance. The weight was of a high value that the whole balance went down. Jlaw and the rest of the people in the court were so amazed and the court became rowdy. At that point, Justinian removed her face covering to see the face of the amazing person that was able to pass her love test for compassion and realized it was the same handsome stranger she had seen earlier.

Just as Justinian was asking the Juslov about himself, the three people who were posed as the oppressed came forward, removed all the mask and costumes they were putting on and then told the princess everything that had happened in the secrete room and how it was only Juslov who showed them compassion. Justinian was very surprised when in all they testified none had mentioned anything about Jlaw's compassion or how he had gotten the diamond so, she turned to Jlaw and asked him how he had gotten the piece of diamond. He tried to lie but then Juslov exposed him.

CHAPTER 8

THE VERDICT

Justinian asked for the other prisoners of love who were in the dungeon to be brought in front of her, and right in front of them she declared Juslov as the one who had won her love test for compassion. Thereafter, she gave her verdict to have the losers beheaded.

On hearing the Justinian verdict, Anna fell down from her sit in shock and died. She was immediately taken out and buried at the noble's tomb.

On seeing all these unexpected events, King Law decided to have mercy on the prisoners of law so, he intervened by reversing Justinian's verdict for the sake of Jlaw.

The king asked for the asked the prisoners to be whipped and imprisoned for five years.

King Law was very happy that his daughter had finally found a good man for herself and decided to get them married in a lavished way.

The whole kingdom went back to their respective homes. Everyone happy and satisfied with all the events that took place in the palace. Most people felt relieved that Anna had passed away because they perceived her as the major negative influence in the life of Jlaw while others just felt pity for her. King Law was also not happy about what happened to Anna but he was very worried about Jlaw.

CHAPTER 9

JUSTINIAN'S TRUE LOVE

King Law summoned Juslov and all his family to appear before him and was surprised to see him with only his mother. Juslov explained to King Law that he had only his mother and no one else so, King Law turned to his mom who came up to introduce herself as Zina.

Zina told King Law everything about her son whose real name was Love. She admitted she had given him the name Juslov to protect him from Anna who was seeking to kill him.

King Law was very shocked to learn all that Anna had done in all these years but he was very happy to know that love his brother's son was alive.

Justinian was also pleased to know more about her would-be husband after which she fell deeply in love with him.

The king gave them both sometime to spend together which gave Love the opportunity to express his love to Justinian. The king threw a grand fairy tale wedding for the two after which they both lived in the palace as prince and princess.

The prince and the princess had sons and daughters there was much happiness in the palace.

Happy Ending

. King Law was happy to see his grand kids and his kingdom at peace,

. Jlaw served his jail term, he repented, became a good human being and he re-united with his half brother. He later inherited his father dukedom.

. Love ascended the throne after the death of King Law, and lived happily with his queen and their kids.

. The people of the legal kingdom loved both the king and the queen and the was peace in the whole kingdom as they lived happily ever after.

THE END!

Your love for me must be tested ---the Justinian's decree!

About The Author

Lawson Motunrayo Auguster is a medical intern, a graduate of botany, a business owner (founder of kingdom Nobles multi-service international). She is a lover of God who had her new birth experience at the age of 10 and has written overcoming the tempter by the unction of the Holy Spirit.